PALM SUNDAY
by Susan C. Barto

FIRST EDITION

Library of Congress Control Number:
2007906757

ISBN-10: 0-9770533-9-3
ISBN-13: 978-0-9770533-9-1

DrurysPublishing.com

Kentucky

Produced in The United States of America.

CONTENTS

CHAPTER 1

FAMILY HISTORY

As usual when they arrived, the table looked gorgeous laden with flowers, the Easter egg name holders, and of course Christine's Lenox. Susan took a good look at the table and at Christine's loving decorations for the holiday before heading with Harry and Bill into the kitchen for a glass of wine. Al sat behind the counter cutting up Italian bread into manageable pieces along with sausage pieces, cheeses, and other traditional Italian goodies to munch before Christine served the antipasto that signaled the start of the almost five hour feast. Bill told all his friends, "You should see Aunt Chris's spread on Palm Sunday and Christmas. The dinner lasts for hours."

Susan, one of five cousins, helped to keep their closeness intact by showing up each Christmas and

Palm Sunday for dinner at Christine's house in Staten Island, New York. The five cousins were children of sisters, two of whom were married to brothers—they felt closely woven. After her cousins' mother died and following the death of Susan's father, Uncle Joe married Susan's mother. This officially made Susan sisters with Andy, Claire and Merry. Christine, the daughter of Susan's mother's twin, already seemed entwined with Susan. Although, Susan only had one actual sibling, her brother, Bill, she had always felt that Andy, Claire, Merry, and Christine were her sisters.

The families celebrated holiday dinners together as long as Susan held memories. Susan married first, and shortly thereafter the other girls married. Soon the holiday dinners included the babies and their assorted high chairs and diaper bags. During her childhood and early married years, Aunt Emily, Mother's twin, and Aunt Marie hosted the events. When the babies grew to be adolescents, Christine began to host the dinners. She had a large house in Staten Island that easily held not only the families, but various friends of the family members. Christine's house's walls seemed to stretch wide enough to include anyone with no place to go. Christine never even had to water the soup, as she cooked enough for an army with leftovers for each to take home.

As the years passed, and the holiday dinners slipped by, changes came and went within the family. Along with the joyous births came the loss of family members. Always the lost ones got toasted with champagne, and Christine kept the food stained name cards of the departed loved ones. Along with grace, homage was always paid to the absent family members, and all acknowledged how they were missed. The holiday parties saw their share of family crises and family dinner table arguments usually over politics. Watergate, Clinton's disgrace, and Bush's failures got debated hotly by the family members.

The five cousins' mothers came from a family of nine children. Their grandparents were born in Italy and descended upon these shores to raise their children and find a new life. Grandpa, one of the success stories of his generation, ended up with several meat packing and shipping trucks. His trucks supplied meat to the big super markets. While his family may not have been rich, they never lacked for meat during the depression. They had steaks and roasts, and they even had their own chickens. While the grandmother and grandfather only learned rudimentary English, the nine children learned English in school and from each other. The twins, Susan knew, spoke impeccable English and could spell up a storm. Eda, Susan's mother, corrected not only Susan's and Bill's English, but the English of their friends much to Susan's annoyance and Bill's embarrassment. One of the nine children died as a baby, but the rest thrived and grew—each different from the other, but they remained close. The oldest two brothers joined Grandpa in the meat business, and legend had it that Mario had ties to the Mafia. Eda used to tell Susan that Uncle Mario ate steak every day, and earned $1000 a week even during the depression.

"Maybe so, Eda, but I loaned him $1,000 once, and I never saw it again."

However Susan's Dad acknowledged that friendship with Mario proved to be important for him as he had the guts to run his warehouse trucks during a Mafia truck strike, and, of course, he was stopped and informed that only his relationship with Mario saved his hide. He put his trucks promptly in a garage and didn't release them until the strike was over. He always said that Mario deserved to keep the $1000 loan. The oldest daughter Margaret contracted spinal meningitis at 2 yrs. of age, and lost her hearing. She subsequently learned to sign and married a deaf man whom she met at her special school. The next daughter, Phyllis, grew to be beautiful and accomplished. She attended Hunter College and became an English teacher. Susan noticed that Eda and Emily never got over their jealousy of Phyllis's having attended college. Next in line, Marie,felt extremely close to Phyllis all her life. Secret family lore informed Susan that Marie had an ill-fated affair with a married man, and when the romance broke up, she dated many men and seemed to have no interest in marriage until her thirty fifth year when she met a Southern gentleman and flipped for his charm. She had a small wedding and a happy, though childless marriage. Aunt Marie adopted all of her nieces and nephews and behaved somewhat like a fairy godmother granting wishes to all. Aunt Marie became the family reporter keeping track of birthdays, anniversaries, and births and deaths. She typed lists with this information and mailed it along with permanent birthday date books to all the cousins encouraging all to keep in touch with each other.

Food and feasts became part of the family tradition. Grandma made and canned her own tomato sauce in the basement of her family home. Lasagna, served at all holidays even Thanksgiving before the turkey, proved to be the favorite. Each of the daughters added their own individual touches to Grandma's original recipe. Even the sauce varied from sister to sister. Aunt Marie, baker to the family, made cheese cakes and chocolate mousse pie along with the traditional chocolate chip cookies and pound and chocolate cakes. She also whipped up a cheese bread—Susan's favorite.

Eda and Emily, the twins, played an ongoing verbal game of ping-pong with each other. This served to spike their competition with each other that needed little spiking. The competition reminded Susan of a ping-pong game because as she observed the twins arguing it appeared to Susan as if first the fight grew because of something Emily said, and the fight expanded and added heat with the next thing Eda said. "Point to Eda here, Point to Emily there," Susan said. They take turns heating up the friction between them. Susan felt as though the twins did not like each other because they saw each other's selfish traits magnified in the twin. Not only did the twins dislike each other, but the twins' husbands hated their wives' twins. "That Emily," Susan's father could be heard to intone, and Frank, Emily's husband could be heard uttering oaths regarding Eda. The whole competition both amused and wearied Susan. Funny to watch as it could be, it also served as fodder for the twins' constant criticism of every other female on the planet. As a child if Susan while watching a movie on television with her mother said, "Isn't she pretty?" Eda would reply "Why shouldn't she be? She can afford spas and plastic surgery."

Indeed, Claire reported that one summer when she visited Eda by her pool in Florida with her small daughter Angela during the time when everyone had fallen in love with Bo Derek in "10" Eda announced "I don't know what's so special about Bo Derek. If I lost 5 pounds, I could look as good as she." As Eda, 70 at the time she uttered this to become memorable line, finished this Claire and Angela had to go under the water in the pool as they howled with laughter. Susan never heard Eda praise another woman's beauty. Susan got further fall out from the twins' competition as she felt that Eda felt jealousy of her that caused her to criticize Susan constantly so as to cause Susan to feel for all of her childhood that she didn't measure up to some standard set only by her Mom. Christine related stories

14

that showed that she suffered similar problems with Emily's apparent competition thing with Eda.

As far as Susan could figure the twins had always been referred to as the twins. In a family of nine, where the twins were neither oldest nor youngest, this must have been difficult. Also the twins, barely five feet tall and unbearably cute, used this attribute to get by on. They were considered so adorable. Men sought their company, and men seemed to find their twin status, attractive. Eda bragged to Susan that all the men Emily dated, including Uncle Frank, whom she married, had liked Eda first. The twins even shared their best friends—Ronnie and Evelyn. Each considered those two her best friends. The four Birra girls—-Phyllis, Marie, Eda and Emily, played lawn tennis in the green Brooklyn parks. They presented an attractive picture in their tennis whites, and they owned their own net as well as the rackets and balls. Men fell all over themselves to compete in tennis with these four girls. The girls always had at least one doubles game going whenever they went to the park with the most handsome men in the park that day. Here is where Eda met Bill, her future husband. Susan felt shocked when she peeked into Eda's diary when Susan herself held the status of a teen. Eda, then a teenager, boasted of her many conquests and how she could handle them. She wrote of them as if they were sex objects or potential wealth objects and referred as to how each could help her get ahead. She noted in the diary that Susan's father made a good appearance and came from a good background as well as being a college bound boy. She had visions of college dances and college weekends. Eda knew and had informed Susan that college men took only the most gorgeous girls to the proms as to be seen with a dog could hurt a reputation and to be seen with a girl upon whom all the stags cut in would be a coup. Naturally, Eda and Emily thought that their beauty would qualify them for many proms and college weekends. They surmised correctly.

"Your Mother," Dad said "always found herself surrounded by men."

Yes, Susan could picture this. According to Eda and Emily, their innocence of things sexual abounded. Eda told Susan a story about how when she at nineteen vacationed at a summer resort hotel, she in all her ignorance went to a man's hotel room never dreaming of danger. Susan found this so hard to believe as her mother and Emily seemed a strange combination of prudery and extreme sexuality and their emotions seemed to see saw between the two extremes. When Eda married Uncle Joe after Dad died, she tried to relate episodes of her love life comparing Uncle Joe and Dad to Susan. "Mother," Susan pleaded. "Enough." Some things seemed not fit for a daughter's ears. Emily, too, appeared to swing back and forth from a sexual being to a prude. When a man tried to have an affair with Susan and she told her mother about it, Eda said, "Oh, I had my first affair when I was 35."

Also stories abounded about kisses from all her sisters' husbands in the large pantry in the suburban Summit house. Susan felt at a loss as to what to believe regarding Eda and Emily and sex. Christine and the cousins reported an equal confusion. Emily shocked the five cousins one summer afternoon when she related having an abortion and said, "Well, it was no big deal. Everyone was doing it then. I don't understand the whole issue."

Susan thought Andy would choke on her spaghetti. Susan, Christine and Andy felt as though you couldn't take the twins anywhere. They kept up a running commentary on the world as though they were watching television and would comment on peoples' appearances when at the mall loudly and with little or no regard to the feelings of those they insulted. Andy, a first grade teacher for many years, handled the twins the best. She would see a fat person heading their way, poke the twins, and say "Eda, Emily, don't you dare."

Harry often chided Susan for not being able to treat her mother the way Andy did. Susan always replied, "It's not the same—she isn't Andy's mother." Susan knew the truth of this as she never felt insulted when Aunt Emily harped at her—indeed she laughed, as she could see from a far better perspective how ridiculous the situation really could be. Andy often said, "I take the twins everywhere, and I don't usually worry. Either people love them or they hate them—I don't take it personally."

CHAPTER 2

FIVE COUSINS

EIGHT COUSINS by Louisa May Alcott. The love existing between Susan and her four cousins represented as close and warm a bond as the more famous EIGHT COUSINS. Andy, their ringleader, the oldest, the most knowing, the one whose opinions counted first and most. Andy's two sisters—blonde and beautiful Claire and dimpled Merry, the baby. And not to be forgotten, Christine, Susan's mother's twin sister's daughter. Their bond ran deeper than blood, and their lasting affection seemed a combination of love between cousins and love between friends. Yes, from an early age, Susan counted herself rich and fortunate with family and friends always at the ready. Happily, she lived in a two-family house in bustling Brooklyn, NY with her brother Bill. Downstairs lived her three cousins, Andy, Claire and Merry. Christine visited nearly every weekend.

Their street life counted as their real life. Here the five cousins including Susan's brother, Bill, held court over the rest of the street. The whole neighborhood perched upon the old green bench in front of their house. In the back of the house stood a black and white dollhouse fashioned by Susan's father and appropriated by Bill for the neighborhood clubhouse. Here they met for meetings. Here Andy discovered that by climbing the lilac tree that touched the clubhouse they could leap onto their garage roof and from their garage roof leap onto all the neighboring roof tops. Here they felt themselves to be kings of all they could survey. On the green bench they played endless games of Truth or Consequences, Time, Charades, and on the black topped smooth streets of the neighborhood they roller skated or jumped rope or rode their bicycles. They taught each other how to ride bikes, no training wheels for them, and how to roller skate. They seemed to manage without adult supervision except, of course, for meals. The older children took charge of their younger charges. They all loved Spaulding pink rubber balls—the girls bounced them playing A is for Alice and other games that required turning the ball over their knee. The boys also loved Spaulding pink balls, they played stoop ball and stick ball. Boys and girls together played endless summer night games of Hide and Seek. The days and evenings were punctuated by the ding of the Good Humor truck. With Uncle Joe around they often got to eat Good Humors both afternoons and evenings as he would buy ice cream for the whole neighborhood in the afternoon and keep mum since he knew they all were allowed only one ice cream per day, choose afternoon or evening.

The street life in Brooklyn wrapped itself around Susan like an Angora blanket, and she felt frightened when her brother and she moved to New Jersey. Devastating for them, but a real coup for their Dad who'd stepped up in the world. Their new home, a red brick Tudor house, on a tree lined street facing an island park filled with cherry trees, looked imposing and a bit scary. Although Susan made friends and learned to fit in here in the strange environment, she lived for visits with the four cousins, either when they drove in to Brooklyn, or when the cousins drove to New Jersey to spend time with Susan and her family. Holidays felt secure and comfortable to Susan since she always spent them with the Brooklyn families. If they traveled there, she wheedled her parents into letting her spend the holiday vacation week in Brooklyn with her cousins. Those vacation weeks seemed magical—a trip back into time and place. For a brief interlude she had her enchanted life back.

When the cousins came to Summit, NJ to visit Susan's family, usually one cousin opted to stay here for a week. Andy and Susan spent one glorious summer week on the screened-in porch reading novels. They each read one or two novels every day. When they reached their teen years, their friendship and bond deepened as they began to date. They shared secrets about their current flames, and arranged dates for each other when they visited each other's homes. Susan arranged numerous double dates for Christine when she visited, and she returned the favor by setting her up with a Brooklyn neighborhood boy upon whom Susan had harbored a crush since childhood and the neighborhood days. When they married they participated in each other's wedding parties. Their children grew up together, and fortunately started out close and remained close into adulthood.

Five cousins they remained, and they felt as close as sisters, Susan knew. No sister could offer more love and support than Susan's four cousins did. When Susan looked at Andy, Claire, Merry, and Christine she saw them at all their ages and stages of development. The laughing young mischief making children skipping rope, climbing roofs and jumping steps melted together and merged into the young married women, happy and sometimes harried mothers, and the more subdued but wiser middle-aged adults they grew to be. Susan thanked God for plunging her into the midst of such a warm and life-embracing family. Life's milestones, joys and sorrows alike when shared become the stuff of memory—memories shared and memories held close to Susan's heart.

CHAPTER 3

NEW YEAR'S EVE

Harry was the only prize Susan ever won. Their meeting started as a fluke when Susan's best friend, Maryann, called just twenty-four hours before New Year's Eve to see whether or not Susan wanted to go on a blind date for the big evening. Maryann knew that Susan had fought with her boyfriend the night before, and therefore, remained dateless. "He won't like you as he's studious and serious, and you're a flake."

"Maryann, you know what you can do with your blind date," Susan rejoined.

At this juncture Maryann's steady, Pete, interrupted with "Of course he'll like you—a sexy terrific girl like you."

Since Pete's blarney never failed to crack Susan up, she relented with a laugh. "Okay, I'll go, but I'd rather stay in my room re-reading GONE WITH THE WIND and listening to Frank Sinatra's "In the Wee Small Hours of the Morning" while the strains of the party my folks are hosting drift up to my room."

Susan's reluctance to go to the party didn't prevent her dressing up fit to kill. She felt determined that this Harry whoever he was would so like her. She wore a black, low-necked cocktail dress enhanced only by a glitter drop in the hollow of her throat. She waited until she heard the doorbell ring before gliding down the long, curving wrought-iron staircase. Harry turned out to have sandy hair and a serious demeanor and appeared shy. They walked out into the icy air, and he said, "I understand that we're both French."

How could he have known that she felt so proud of her half-French heritage? She wanted to go to Paris and loved everything French. She warmed to him instantly, and they started to bond. Once at the party, however, dancing commenced. Harry, to her surprise, didn't invite Susan to dance so when another boy did, she started to dance. At midnight she returned to Harry, and they shared a kiss. The kiss proved to be so perfect that they followed it with another to the apparent shock of one of Harry's friends who didn't bother to hide his disapproval. After the kiss Susan felt sure he'd ask her to dance, but once again he did not. The boy she'd danced with before sought her out, and they danced again. After the dance she returned looking for Harry only to learn that he'd gone out on the porch. She grabbed her wrap and went out on the porch looking for him, sure that she'd not imagined all the good vibes between them. She found him smoking a cigarette in this frigid night.

"Sue, what are you doing out here?"

"You're my date. I followed you out here."

"Why? Weren't you enjoying your dance?"

"No, I wanted to dance with you. Why didn't you ask me?"

"My dancing is rotten. I rarely dance until I know a girl really well."

"Well you should have shared that information with me. It confused me, I thought you didn't like me."

"Our midnight kiss should have dispelled that fear. That's why I felt confused."

After the explanations concluded, they began talking. In the two hours out in the winter night they discussed their whole lives prior to their meeting. Susan learned that Harry had been Catholic like her, but had left the Church. However, he quickly added to this, "Once a Catholic, always a Catholic."
Susan felt relieved by this, but she didn't know why. A thought flew into her head, unbidden, that this would be the man she would marry. The thought puzzled her, and she knew enough to keep this crazy notion to herself. When they finally turned to go back into the party, they noticed people spilling

out the door into the night heading for home. They hurried back in to thank their hosts, found Maryann and Pete and walked to the car. On the way home in the back seat, Harry kissed her, and she reached up to touch his hair that felt as soft as a paint brush. She felt as if she rode in Cinderella's pumpkin coach, and that like Cinderella her life had just begun.

CHAPTER 4

MARRIAGES

Susan, to her shock, married first at eighteen. Her first instincts about Harry proved to be true, and her love for him never wavered. Dad expressed shock and displeasure about her marrying so young.

"Harry, I like you, and I am in favor of your marrying Susan. However, you have graduated college, and Susan has yet to begin her college education. If she does not get her degree you will in later years as you rise in business be ashamed of her."

"Dad," Harry replied, "I could never be ashamed of Susan. She is smart and talented, and with her love of literature she will go to college even if she has to take one course at a time."

At this juncture Mother chimed in and in usual Eda fashion chirped, "Bill, you better let Susan marry Harry, she may not get another chance."

With a loving set of parents like this, Susan felt she needed no enemies. However, Harry who showed Susan what love could be handled everything with aplomb, and Susan sat back and tried to let him handle the situation. With a deftness and tact she wouldn't have believed possible he managed to sooth Dad, and for the moment at least wedding plans could go forward. The family began to plan a July wedding—a hotel chosen for the reception—now Susan and Harry could go and visit the Priest. Unfortunately, the visit to Susan's Parish Priest took an unpleasant and unexpected turn. Harry's having been Catholic at birth, agreed to marry in the Catholic Church although he had turned Presbyterian a year or two ago. Susan felt great relief knowing that her parents would be devastated if she didn't marry in the Church. Father Murray had a nice talk with the two of them, and as they were getting ready to depart dropped the bombshell. "You know, of course," he said "that you will have to sign a document with your hand on the Bible saying that you will never use birth control."

"Father," Susan said. "We can't sign such a document. We know that we do not want to have 10 children."

"Susan, go home and think about it," said Father Murray.

Susan, faced with a dilemma of fearsome proportions, meandered home with Harry and dreaded the meeting with her folks. Harry tried to cheer her up, and went home as the dinner hour approached and Susan's Dad's arrival loomed. After her parents had both sat down at the dinner table, Susan and her brother Bill joined them. Susan had already filled Bill in on the problem. "Daddy," Susan began,

"Father Murray said that he will not marry us unless I sign a document with my hand on the Bible saying that I will never practice birth control. I cannot sign such a document."

"Oh, Susan, I understand how you feel. However, if you do not marry in the Catholic Church, I will not attend your wedding."

"Oh, Bill you don't mean that," Mother said.

"I know that Susan feels that she would be a hypocrite by signing that document, and I agree with her, but if she does not sign it, I repeat I will not attend the wedding."

Susan felt struck with grief. This hit hard especially since Dad did not attend Church, and Mother did. Interesting, that Mother would attend the marriage even if they married in another Church but that Dad wouldn't. Where could there be logic to this? Susan decided to postpone any decision for the time being. She tabled the discussion at least for that evening and said, "Daddy, I'll think and pray about it."

Two days later when Susan arrived home from Katherine Gibbs where she attended secretarial school, a choice she'd made instead of college for the time being, Mother greeted her with these words, "The Monsignor of the Church called and said that you should sign the document and then go to confession."

Susan felt devastated. What kind of edict had the Monsignor proposed. It sounded like such hypocrisy to Susan. Being as idealistic as she would ever be in her life, and she thought, Heaven help those who are not idealistic at 18, she faced a quandary. Now in the month of February plans regarding the proposed wedding had been going on since around Christmas when Harry proposed. Already Dad and Mother quarreled nightly as to whom would be invited to the wedding. "I only have one relative, Cousin Rudy," and if he's not invited you can't have your huge family," Dad had said only last week. Mother had rejoined with "Your cousin Rudy means nothing to me, and he's not coming."

Susan faced more months of this along with her Dad's ultimatum about not attending the wedding if she chose to marry in the Presbyterian Church, Harry's Church of choice. She contemplated all her options and came up wanting. After conferring with Harry together they decided to marry within three or four weeks even though she had not graduated from Katherine Gibbs. Somehow they would find a way for her to finish, locate an apartment, and start their own lives. Harry came to this decision the night that Susan's Dad pulled the telephone plug out of the wall in a rage over wedding plans and the

Church of choice, and he managed to convince Susan that for her sanity this would be the only option.

Susan visited Harry's Church and planned her wedding. As soon as the date had been firmed up, she told her family. Mother went along, invited her relatives, and shopped for a new dress. Dad planned a business trip so that he could stick to his threat of not attending if the wedding did not take place in the Catholic Church. Susan and Harry delved into finding the apartment and all the sundry things that loomed over their heads, and Susan continued doing five hours of homework a night. Love propelled Susan to reserves of energy she didn't know she possessed. In three weeks, a small wedding had been planned. Her friends at Katherine Gibbs threw her a wedding shower, her relatives planned to attend, her Uncle Joe planned to give her away, and Susan felt joy in spite of the adverse circumstances. Her love for Harry never wavered even in the midst of all the turmoil surrounding them. They found a tiny apartment close enough to where Harry could commute and Susan could finish her few more months of school. They had already purchased a bedroom grouping of furniture months ago, and they managed to buy or borrow enough to finish furnishing the apartment.

The night before her wedding, also the night of her shower, her father who'd finished packing and was about to leave for the airport stuck his head into her bedroom where she pretended to sleep. He told her inert form that he loved her and was sorry. However, he left as planned. Susan never stirred from her pretended sleep. On her honeymoon a telegram came from Dad saying "May you always be as happy as you are now" along with a dozen red roses." The war with Dad seemed to have ended, but Susan felt stung by his not attending the wedding that in every other respect fulfilled all her expectations. In fact, in later years when she and Harry attended lavish weddings they recalled their small one when all they wanted to do was leave and be alone for their weekend honeymoon. Indeed, they left as soon as decently possible, and spent a deluxe weekend in a fancy New York City hotel, hitting the shows and restaurants and luxuriating in each other's company. Her best wedding present or shower present came from the girls in her class who did all her homework for the weekend that they could get away with. Anything that needed her handwriting, Susan did herself on Sunday night. Susan's honeymoon and wedding would remain in her mind as the best weekend of her life, and her love and joy in her husband never wavered for 42 years. After three years, Susan gave birth to their precious son, Billy.

CHAPTER 5

ANDY GETS MARRIED

Andy had been in love with Rich before Susan even met Harry. In fact, Andy's choice of Rich seemed to exemplify the choices the other cousins would make. Rich's honest and nice persona became the example the other men in the family would have to live up to. Rich possessed good looks as well as a gentle but strong manliness. Susan felt proud that Harry, too, possessed this quality. She brought Harry to a family reunion to win Andy's approval - something that seemed important. Andy and Rich attended Wagner College in Staten Island together. Andy had begun college at sixteen and met Rich shortly thereafter. Susan remembered that the first time she heard about Rich she herself had been enamored of an eighth grade boy named Chuck whom Andy met and of whom Andy approved. Andy's approval went a long way with Susan. Susan felt delighted that Andy approved the choice of her heart. One stormy night right after Andy had met Chuck during a rare sleep over at Susan's house as the two girls lay in bed watching the lightening and listening to the thunder, Andy began talking about Rich. She talked about all the college things they did together like football games and dances. She also laughed and mentioned a late night game they played called buttons—a form a strip polka without the deck of cards.

Andy, although just sixteen, attended Wagner College. She had graduated from high school at a scant sixteen—after having skipped a couple of grades. Susan at this time, felt even younger than her fourteen years compared to her college coed cousin. Her high school exploits paled in comparison to Andy's college experiences. However, Susan's crush on Chuck ran so deep that high school seemed okay to her at this moment in time. All through her young life Susan tried to emulate Andy in every aspect that she could. Andy seemed to embody perfection in a teenager that Susan longed for. In fact, leave it to Andy's Mom, Susan's adored Aunt Phyllis, to send her a "Now you are a Teenager" card on her 13th birthday. If Andy approved of Susan's choice of reading matter, boyfriend, or new outfit, it won raves from Susan. Susan adored Andy. Andy teased Susan unmercifully, and reigned supreme over all five cousins.

Susan's wedding to Harry actually took place before Andy's wedding to Rich, although Andy and Rich comprised the first official couple in the family. Andy's unofficial engagement to Rich traveled the family gossip network long before Susan's official engagement to Harry. When Susan attended Andy and Rich's wedding, she had been married over a year. She wore a raspberry silk dress, and felt quite a sexy young married woman. Andy's wedding proved to be the last time the entire family were together as a whole—before Aunt Phyllis died and before the untimely deaths of other family members. Susan remembered the wedding as a happy time. She and Harry sat at the cousins' table, and Harry even did the fast dances aided by the champagne. Harry always needed alcohol before doing the Lindy—otherwise, he directed his good friends to do the fast dances with Susan. Susan recalled that Andy, Claire, and Merry called their Mother Marmie as in "Little Women." They always spoke to and about her with so much love, and Susan agreed. She couldn't imagine loving anyone as much as she loved her Aunt Phyllis. That afternoon during the height of the wedding, Aunt Phyllis ambled over to their table to see how the cousins were enjoying the wedding. After much talk and laughter she returned to her own table, and Claire crooned, "Sweet, fat, Marmie." Susan knew how much love entered into this statement. Aunt Phyllis, although by far the prettiest of all the Birra women, struggled with her weight without much success. All to the delight of

Eda and Emily, who managed to keep their weight in bounds.

Shortly after their wedding, Andy and Rich moved to East Orange where Susan and Harry lived—a short two or three blocks from them. This proved advantageous as Andy would often call and say, "Come over. I feel like comfortable company." On hot summer late Sunday afternoons, she would call and say, "Let's escape to an air-conditioned movie. I have to get out of this heat." However, Andy would last about three or four minutes before complaining to Richie, "I'm freezing, give me your sweater." Susan always chuckled because she never felt the cold even in the sub-zero temperatures of the winter. Each Christmas season Andy would call and invite Susan and Harry over so that they could write Christmas cards together, and once in a while the guys went out, and the girls stayed home and had a girl's night. They took each other to their favorite pizza places comparing the various pies.

This foursome lasted until Susan got pregnant, and she and Harry moved to New Providence—a town Susan felt better suited to bring up a family. Shortly, thereafter Andy and Rich moved away to another part of New Jersey and bought their first house. When Susan and Harry's son reached two years old, they, too, bought their first house. Andy and Rich had two boys—the first boy, Robert, born only a year after Susan's Bill had been born. Andy and Rich's second boy, Paul, was born soon after. Andy's family now seemed complete—even perfect. Andy's and Rich's second house lay situated in the wooded section of a lovely old town. Unfortunately, it was too far away from Susan's and Harry's house for them to visit as often or as impromptu as they used to. But visits among all the cousins remained special—they always got together for Palm Sunday and for Christmas. Once in a while, Susan and her Mother would drive to Andy's with Billy when he was small, and Billy would play with Andy's boys. Bill stayed in the terrible two's longer than Andy's boys did. So, the first time Andy invited Billy to stay the night proved to be the last time she extended the invitation. Among his other tricks, Bill said, "My Mommy lets me keep the radio on all night," Andy had to agree to let the wily toddler keep the radio blaring all night.

Andy and Rich had a good, strong marriage that lasted almost forty years. She and Rich both worked in the school systems—Andy taught first grade, and Rich worked in the administrative end as a counselor and also a principal. After both retired they moved to Florida to be near Andy's father. Uncle Joe had by this time married Susan's mother after Susan's father died, and seven years after Aunt Phyllis' untimely death. Sadly, Rich became ill with cancer and died before they had really settled in. This death came shortly on the heels of Uncle Joe's death, and Rich did not live to see his new grandchild. However, he fortunately, knew of the coming of his first grandchild. Merry had lost her 49 year old husband a couple of years before, and now both

Merry and Andy were widows. Andy and Merry, however, kept on with their busy lives, and carried on. Merry's John and Rich would never be forgotten in the family lore. In fact, each Palm Sunday the family toasted all its absent loved ones. Rich's first grandchild, Nolan, looked just like Rich. The family rejoiced.

CHAPTER 6

CHRISTINE MARRIES AL

Christine dated boys named Al. She did so with such frequency that even Susan's brother, Bill, noted the fact. Susan had been married almost five years before Christine finally chose an Al to marry. Before this final Al entered her life, no one had been handsome enough or had enough personality. Susan arranged many blind dates for Christine, and although most of the guys liked Christine, she never completely approved of any of these dates. Susan had begun to wonder whether or not she could be too fussy to ever marry.

However, when the final Al entered her life, Christine fell quickly and hard. A football star at Wagner College where she as had most of the girls in the family attended, he had long harbored a crush on her and had finally managed to arrange a first date. It seemed at first, according to the legend that reached Susan, a mismatch. Indeed, Christine felt in the mood to be driven home immediately after dinner with its stilted attempts at conversation. However, on the way home, Al proposed that the two go someplace to dance and Christine reported having been intrigued. Christine later related that she would rather dance than eat, and felt surprised and later delighted that Al, too, loved to dance. Dancing did it. As in the song "Shall we Dance" from "The King and I" Christine and Al became hopelessly enamored after dancing. Christine told Susan, "Al danced like a prince." When Susan's brother, Bill, heard of Christine's engagement he asked Susan, "Is his name Al?"

Al and Christine, too, worked on Wall Street with its frantic pace. They eventually had two children, Mark and Dana, and resided in Staten Island and in an apartment in New York City during the week. They had an apartment in Marco Island, Florida as a vacation retreat. Shortly after their children became toddlers, Christine began to take over the holidays dinners after her mother, Emily, stopped. The famous Palm Sunday and Christmas dinners took place at Christine's and Al's in Staten Island. Christine's dinners followed in the hallowed footsteps of Aunt Marie in Long Island and her own mother Emily. All but Emily loved Christine's lasagna even more than Aunt Emily's lasagna. In fact, all Christine's cooking proved superb and without peer except for the family's united opinion that Emily's famous meatballs had no equal. Christine, too, agreed with this decision. However, Emily bestowed no such equal compliments upon Christine's marvelous cooking and hosting skills. In fact, she complained about the sauce being cold, the lasagna over-cooked, the noodles being the wrong size, etc. One famous Palm Sunday, she announced over dinner, "These lasagna noodles are larger than the ones I use."

Long-suffering Al, her son-in-law, said without missing a beat, "I was up all night stretching them." Indeed, all Christine's children and eventually grandchildren chimed in on this rather nasty competition of Emily's. One year after Emily had complained bitterly about last Palm Sunday's sauce being cold, Mark dropped this last into the conversation as the family enjoyed the lasagna, "Ma, the sauce is so hot I am burning my tongue." All, but Emily laughed. Subtle remarks fell on deaf ears in Emily's and also Eda's case.

Dana, Christine's beautiful daughter, became the first child of the cousins to marry. Christine and Al hosted a lavish wedding at the New York Athletic Club, and the family rejoiced. Mark's marriage followed soon after. Swiftly, Christine and Al became the first grandparents in the family. Tragedy would not escape Christine's and Al's lovely family, either. The World Trade Center tragedy touched this little family who lost Dana's Denis when one of their two girls was three and the other six months.

Once again the family threw its arms around Dana and the whole family. Once again the family's combined strength reached toward Dana.

CHAPTER 7

MERRY MARRIES

When Merry fell in Love with John, two men fell in love with Merry, Susan observed when seeing the trio together. John and his twin, Louis, both felt head over heels about Merry, and lavished double helpings of attention upon her whenever they all got together. Merry met John at Wagner, where she, too, went to college. John, like Al whom he knew, a football hero, courted Merry with Louis' approval. To Susan, it seemed like Scarlett and the Tarleton twins in GONE WITH THE WIND. May the best brother win, and the other would be delighted that his other half had won the prize. Actually, Susan noted, it took Louis a lot of years before he married. Until then, Merry seemed to have acquired two men of her own.

Merry looked the most like her mother, Phyllis. Phyllis had been the reigning beauty in a handsome family. When Merry hit her thirties and went to visit an old neighbor of Phyllis' the neighbor, Rose, thought she was seeing the ghost of Phyllis and became disconcerted. Then, too, Merry like her mother became a kindergarten teacher. Susan knew from first hand experience how wonderful a teacher Aunt Phyllis was—she had taught Susan how to read when at the age of four she could hardly hold some of the heavy books she wanted to read. Given that Susan often needed to escape from the turbulence in her family, she took to reading like a cat to cream. She devoured the Bobbsey Twin books before finishing first grade, and had read JANE EYRE when only in the sixth grade. In fact, her teacher felt so proud of this twelve year old reader in his class that he pointed her out as the little woman who had read JANE EYRE to any passing visitor to the class.

Merry taught kindergarten for many years in New York, New Jersey and Florida. John coached a baseball team in his spare time. Merry and John had three handsome children—Laura, John, and Tina. All three looked somewhat like their beautiful mother. One memorable summer, Susan, Andy, Merry (before she became a mother herself) and Susan's mother right after marrying Uncle Joe vacationed for two weeks in Florida. A special vacation, enhanced by the visit of Aunt Marie and Uncle Herb from Alabama for a few days. This proved to be a fine opportunity for Susan's Billy to bond with

Andy's Robert and Paul. This pleased Susan as she wanted her children to be close to the children of her cousins as she had been close to their parents. The summer created an adventure as the sea turtles were laying their eggs on the beach that month. Andy, Susan and Merry kept up a pilgrimage each evening lying in wait for a turtle to begin laying. Finally after a few fruitless nights they watched in silence as a mother sea turtle laid over 100 eggs on the beach crying tears as she did so and then when finished she got up and lumbered into the sea where her loyal mae waited.

Eda had a friend who watched over the eggs and helped the baby turtles to journey safely over the sand into the sea to commence their young lives. With luck, sea turtles if they survive babyhood live long lives. This vacation seemed marred to Susan only by Billy's few temper tantrums. He had entered the tantrum age, and she knew enough to stand silently by until he had completed the display of temper. She neither gave in to an unreasonable demand or lost her cool. Merry and Andy gazed at this fireworks display with wonder. They all went to the fireworks on the beach on the Fourth of July, and Merry provided a feast including Susan's guilty favorite—devil dogs. That summer the young women were young enough to both attract attention from some young men on the beach who watched more than turtles and to wallow in silly fears over snakes, a favorite fear with Susan, thunderstorms, Merry's, and a reported rapist seen in the area, Andy's. They took long walks on the beach and to a local Howard Johnson's for forbidden afternoon ice cream cones and took the children to lion safari. Merry was joined at one point by Louis rather than John. Louis claimed to have been in the area.

Merry's John had to make several moves. They lived in a few places in New Jersey, then in Ohio, and finally moved to Florida where they were joined by Eda and Joe and Andy and Rich. Sadly, Merry's John died of a heart attack when he hit his 49th year. He had had a scare a little earlier, and had put his affairs in order. Merry kept on keeping on teaching and bringing up the three children who were at that time in their late teens.

CHAPTER 8

CLAIRE SHOCKS THE FAMILY AND HAS A CINDERELLA ENDING

Claire, the only blonde in the family and judged by most to be the most gorgeous with her Madonna-like beauty. She dated a lot—from junior high school on. She had an easy, relaxed manner when talking to men. This attribute coupled with her blonde beauty made her a favorite with most men on the planet. She never had trouble talking with men. She reminded Susan of her girlfriend Betty who was born knowing how to talk to men—a fact Susan attributed to her having two older brothers. Claire, however, grew up in a house full of women, albeit popular women. Aunt Phyllis had set the standard—apparently so popular in her youth, that Uncle Joe claimed she chose him because he was the only man with whom she didn't fall asleep from boredom sometime during the date. Claire met a handsome man named Christos in her twenties. Chris, as everyone called him, hailed from Greece and spoke with a Greek accent that only added to his considerable charms. Claire and Chris moved in together in an era where this was not common. Uncle Joe, the original free spirit, seemed okay with this" After all," he said, "They are over twenty-one." However, Aunt Marie felt shocked. "I will not speak to that man, she uttered. "I will write to and communicate with Claire, but I will have nothing to do with that man."

Aunt Marie set herself up as judge to various things within the family. Childless herself, she considered the cousins to be her own children. Something that gave a good deal of pleasure to all concerned. The cousins adored her—she cooked better than anyone in the family and hosted many of the lavish family feasts before Christine and Emily did. She was the original baker in the family— Claire learned her skills from Aunt Marie, and the luscious desserts Claire baked for the family feasts came from Aunt Marie's recipes. Claire and Chris lived together happily for a while in spite of the shock waves that reverberated among the stricter members of the family including Susan's father who disapproved of most everything. When they decided upon having a family they had a quiet wedding, and all seemed forgiven by Aunt Marie and the rest of the ones who had whispered. In Aunt Marie's case shouted would be more correct.

Claire and Chris lived in Manhattan and were the most savvy and cosmopolitan of the cousins. Susan felt jealous that Claire could go ice skating and see the tree at Rockefeller Center and watch the Thanksgiving parade and even the wild Halloween parade to say nothing of being in the midst of the political background in New York. Claire loved to shop and managed to get designer label products for all for bargain rates. In fact, for a while Claire became a buyer for one of the large New York department stores. During this period, Susan adored the Christmas presents Claire could obtain for the cousins, and Susan looked forward to opening Claire's always gorgeous gifts. Claire gave birth to a beautiful daughter, Angela. The song "Angie Baby" was popular at that time, and Claire managed to have the local NY radio station play the song for baby Angela. She spoke to the DJ.

CHAPTER 9

MY BOY BILL

Susan gave birth to Bill when she hit twenty-one years old—according to the books the most healthy age to give birth for both mother and child. She and Harry looked forward with joy to the baby's birth. As Bill's birth took place on January 16th, Susan felt very pregnant by Christmas time. Although Dad always teased her saying, "There is no such thing as a little bit pregnant." That Christmas Claire looked at Susan and Harry, smiled and said, "What a lucky baby to be so wanted and welcomed into this world."

Aunt Marie had hosted a baby shower for Susan at her home on Thanksgiving when, naturally, the whole family had gathered. Susan feigned surprise, but she had had suspicions and Dad had slipped by saying, "You looking forward to the shower?"

After those words had been spoken, Susan put two and two together and came up with Thanksgiving for the baby shower. It did not spoil the shower for her, and she hoped it did not spoil the shower for those who may have suspected that she was not overwhelmed with surprise. Susan's girlfriends threw her another baby shower, and Bill would have his own room that Susan and Harry kept busy decorating and adorning with mint green and yellow curtains with ducks and all the necessary crib plus equipment. Harry's sister, Joan, provided a tiny cradle that Susan placed in the master bedroom so she could keep a watch over the baby for the first few weeks. Bill had a normal and happy birth, and when Susan looked at him for the first time and saw that white blond angel hair, she felt enchanted. It seemed like love at first glance, and Susan became unable to read about the horror stories that newspapers provided about child abuse, abandonment or even murder of a child by the parents. She cringed and had to go grab Bill. Soon she stopped reading the Metro section of the New York Times altogether.

Bill turned out to be an amazing and good infant, skipping his two-o-clock in the morning feeding after just two weeks. He enjoyed the walks in the new carriage Susan had coveted since her childhood, and he drank his milk and took his naps. His crying time fortunately came around 6 p.m., and he had fallen asleep long before Susan's and Harry's bedtime. Late night television, especially old movies, had just come into being, and Susan spent many an early morning feeding Bill on the couch accompanied by old classic movies. Bill's perfect childhood lasted until he entered the terrible two's. Susan could often be heard to say, "The terrible two's are supposed to give way to the charming three's but Bill stayed in the terrible two's until fifth grade."

Bill looked forward to starting school—watching the first day of school parade from Susan's front yard each year. One year he even joined the first day of school parade marching to the school in his little red bathrobe with Susan frantic and following behind him in her little blue Volkswagon until the vice-principal caught up with him, and turned him over to his harried mother. However, Bill developed problems with schooling early on getting himself expelled from Nursery School, on probation in first grade, and suspended from the second grade. Susan dreaded the ringing of the telephone on school days, as the principal often called to ask her to come and take Bill home as he had disrupted the class again. Andy suggested, "Susan, just don't answer the phone during school hours. You are not at home. They could not get away with this with working mothers."

Then began Susan's and Harry's battle with the school officials as to where Bill should be placed within the school system. For a while he entered special classes with learning disabled children, and shortly reentered the regular school system He did not, however, begin to like school until his junior and senior year in high school. When he graduated from high school Eda and Uncle Joe traveled from Florida and hosted a huge graduation party for Bill. Susan said with amazement to Eda, "When I graduated high school I just got a watch, not a party and all this fuss."

Eda replied, "Yes, but we never thought Bill would get out of school."

Those words proved to be a foreshadowing as Bill loved Seton Hall, the University he attended, so much that he never wanted to leave college. He went on to earn three Masters degrees and a Doctorate degree from Drew University. He became a college professor in a small community college in up State New York—part of SUNY. He was loved by the entire town— professors and students alike. He even advertised the college on the radio, became a volunteer in the adult literacy program, displayed his collection of old fashioned record players to the kindergarten and grade school children, and otherwise entered the life of his little town. Bill seemed to have found his niche in life, and seemed well pleased. Susan and Harry just about burst with pride over his achievements.

CHAPTER 10

TRAGEDY STRIKES

Just when life seemed to be spinning along quite nicely for Susan—she and Harry had been married 41 years and Bill had settled into college town life as a professor—tragedy struck. It started as a pretty normal Sunday—one Susan had looked forward to as she and Harry would be picking Bill up at the airport after having visited his closest friend and the boy Susan called her second son Tom in Michigan where Tom had just moved in order to take a tenure track job as a history professor. Bill's mission in visiting Tom had been to bring Tom's beloved cat, Quasi. Bill also managed to locate a good Italian restaurant for Tom and help him buy some new furniture for his apartment. Susan and Harry greeted Bill, took him to the house to unpack and the three headed out to their favorite Japanese restaurant for dinner. Bill told them that he enjoyed spending weekends with them. In fact, once in a while he'd say when coming for a visit, "Don't tell my friends I'll be home, let's just spend the weekend together the three of us."

The trip to the Japanese restaurant seemed something of a pilgrimage to Susan. Bill loved Japanese food, and the three of them loved this restaurant enough to travel three quarters of an hour to have dinner there. That Sunday evening they had been gathered together around the piano singing a song for which Bill had obtained the sheet music. He seemed anxious for Susan to learn to play it as it included the theme music to one of their favorite movies—THE APARTMENT. They attended the Japanese restaurant so often that the hostess greeted them with a smile and always led them to the choicest table available. On the way home they stopped at the video store for a new video to watch that evening. Susan remembered that they were laughing. It became her very last memory before waking up and seeing their new car shattered and Bill and Harry motionless in the car. She had vivid memories of thinking this is the worst thing that ever happened to us. She then turned to her left where she lay pinned next to her son, her seat had been thrown into the back seat alongside her child. She looked at her beloved child and saw an angel. She knew immediately that he was dead, and that his spirit already had flown to Heaven. She could see

Harry, and he seemed to be unconscious, but she knew that he remained alive. She began to pray frantically for Harry to live. For the rest of her life she would feel guilty that she had not prayed for Bill, but just prayed for God to let Harry live.

"He never knew or felt anything," the doctors told Susan about Bill. After an autopsy had been performed, she learned that he had died instantly. Thank God, she thought. Perhaps the darkest day of her life Susan had to have Bill cremated according to his wishes. Bill's friends got together and brought a Priest to the funeral home to say prayers over Bill before the cremation. One of Bill's close friends left his fiancée at home with Susan while the rest went to the funeral home.

"I do not advise that the Mother come to the funeral home to see her child after an autopsy has been performed," said the funeral director. Susan's shocked state let her obey this edict, and she and Karen stayed at home. When the Priest and Bill's friends arrived back at the house they told funny anecdotes about Bill, but Susan did not feel ready to hear them. She declined their offer to accompany them to a Chinese restaurant for dinner, but asked Karen to bring her back some Wonton soup. For weeks after Bill's death Susan subsisted on soup—the hot liquid being the only nourishment that she could manage to swallow. Tom stayed with Susan for a few days, and his presence gave her a small measure of strength. Susan cousins, Christine, Claire, Andy and Merry became her support system. The evening of the tragedy as Susan lay in the hospital a minister came to her and asked, "Whom do you want to call?"

"I'll call my cousin, Claire, and my friend Gini."

Claire and her cousin Christine and Claire's husband Christos arrived at the hospital before Susan received the official news that Bill had died. Susan called Gini, her close friend, on the phone and said,

"Gini, I think Bill is dead."

"Sue, you don't know that."

"Oh, but I do, Gini."

Gini led a parade and an army of Susan's friends who led her through her state of shock and managed along with Harry's and Bill's friends to get her to the hospital to see Harry each day as he lay hovering over death in a coma. Susan got up, got dressed— albeit skipping makeup—and walked around in a trance. She only felt that life had a purpose when she was on the way to visit Harry. She lived for these visits and she never doubted that he would survive. The third day as he lay in the coma, a male nurse let slip in a callus and off-hand fashion that "Your husband is going to die anyway even if he gets out of the coma from the cancer."

"What cancer?" 'Susan asked horrified.

She turned to the doctors who confirmed the news they had delayed imparting to her that an old cancer of Harry's had returned and had metastasized. Susan telephoned the cancer specialist and inquired as to how long Harry could live. "Does he have two years?"

"Yes, maybe a lot more."

Harry proceeded to wake from the coma, and go to a rehab. There he learned how to walk, talk, and swallow again. He suffered brain damage, but fortunately he recovered on the high side. He, thank God, Susan thought retained his essential core of sweetness. Susan's life had changed forever—no longer existed their little trio against the world. Rather, Susan had to face and prepare herself for a life alone. However, she determined to keep Harry alive as long as humanly possible and to nurse him back to health so far as she could. When she got him home, an army of therapists descended upon the household, and Harry slowly gained strength. Susan fed him nourishing meals and he regained the 60 pounds he had lost in the hospital. She collected the cancer slides from his old cancer and took him to the best oncologist in the area. Harry began chemotherapy that fortunately did not ever make him sick.

Susan allowed herself to hope. The oncologist opened a window on her despair by saying, "This kind of cancer responds well to chemo." At last, Susan began to think that Harry might live for the five years and see a few Christmas trees and eat a few Feast of Stephen rib roast dinners. In addition to the stream of therapists coming daily to the house, Susan took Harry to a rehab daily for physical and cognitive therapy. Harry often said, "I know I have cancer, but I feel so well I hope we can go back to Egypt and go to Texas to see my mother."

This became what Susan lived for. To get Harry to Egypt one last time, and to first stop in Texas to visit his mother who had been so brave all during this never ending ordeal. Susan thanked God for their having visited as a family Italy and London, and as a couple Paris three times and Egypt twice. They had their love of travel in common, and the trips had enhanced their joy in each other and in their marriage. These memories remained locked in the family memory bank and could never be dislodged as long as Susan lived. For that matter, as long as Susan lived and held the memories of her loved ones locked in her heart they could never die.

Indeed it seemed as though their dreams of one last trip could come true. On one routine visit to the oncologist he said, "The cancer has gone from the chest because of the chemo, but I see something on the liver."

Susan stumbled onto a bench in the doctor's office and let her tears spill. She had banked all her hopes on Harry's cancer shrinking, and having this wonderful man in her life for at least another five years. She had held inside her how serious his condition was and told Harry, "You have survived cancer four times before, you will conquer this too."

Susan remembered Memorial Day weekend as the beginning of the end. On that fateful weekend Harry had a seizure. Susan drove him immediately to the hospital, where a cat scan showed that the cancer had spread to his brain. Now the cancer ate away at his brain and liver. The doctors recommended radiation to the brain, and Susan agreed having no idea what lay in store. The first day of the radiation Susan and Harry went out to their usual haunt for dinner, and Harry ate three pork chops, potato and veggies and a dish of strawberry ice cream. After one week of radiation to the brain he could no longer sit up by himself. Unfortunately, he had to enter the hospital and from there a nursing home for rehab in order to get him to sit up and walk so that he could return home to die. Susan spent every waking moment at the rehab center taking care of Harry—trying to get him to eat, nursing him through two bouts of pneumonia, and assisting in the therapy to get him walking. However, in spite of her best efforts to get him on his feet to go to Texas to see his Mom and then to Egypt one last time, he died. Harry died within six days after the first anniversary of Bill's death. Susan felt bereft. She did not really feel as though she had anything to live for, but got up each day and put one foot in front of the other and continued. Her writing and work at the Art Museum saved her life. She began an active social live, and even developed a crush that lasted two years on a man she met in the diner where she had dinner each evening.

CHAPTER 11

AFTER THE TRAGEDY

Susan kept on keeping on for seven years after the death of her precious son and husband. She joined Weight Watchers and a gym and got herself fit and trim. She took on a more important job at the Museum as the Volunteer Coordinator, and got several books published and had a book signing. Life continued. Thank God for Susan she had Tom in her life. Tom, Bill's best friend, had always been her second son. He told Susan "On the day that Bill was cremated, I promised him that I would take care of his parents." Tom never once wavered from this startling commitment. Susan felt blessed by his caring. Tom traveled with her to Staten Island for Christmas and Palm Sunday whenever possible. Susan never had to spend a Thanksgiving, Easter, or

Christmas alone thanks to Tom. Susan knew that Bill and Harry watched over her in Heaven and knew that Tom had taken her under his formidable wing. Susan even attended a Great Books class at Seton Hall where Bill graduated and taught. She got an A on the mid-term, on her paper, and on her final exam.

Palm Sundays and Christmas holidays continued at Christine's. However, just recently Christine and Al put their house on the market, and it appears as though the family dinners will continue at Dana's large house in Cherry Hill, New Jersey. This makes it difficult for Susan to attend, but Christine still hosts dinners until she manages to sell the house. Palm Sunday—the tapestry upon which Susan's and the lives of her cousins were woven—continued. Susan thanked God for her family—especially her four cousins. Five cousins they remained through all that life had in store. Susan looked forward to reaching old age in concert with her four cousins.

CHAPTER 12

POLITICS

Also woven into the tapestry of her life, politics proved a vital element to the equation. When Bill was a youngster in grade school Susan became the executive secretary to the Republican Party in Union County. She also became a Legislative Aide to a State Senator. Harry became a councilman in their town. Politics posed the first and only threat to their marriage. Amoral behavior especially extra-marital affairs ran rampant through out the County where Susan worked. One of the men running for County office tried to have an affair with Susan. Harry quit the council, Susan quit all her political activities, and they moved out of the County to the country. Susan's fascination with politics remained a lifelong passion in which she indulged by watching cable news year round for campaign news. Watching political news still can get her out of a slump. During her tenure in politics Susan threw a fund raiser for George Bush, Sr. Her prize possessions include a picture with herself and George and Barbara Bush and herself with Jack Kemp. She and Harry were invited to the swearing in ceremonies, parties and balls for both President Nixon and President Reagan. She follows political news with a fervent interest, and reads the New York Times each day for news of the candidates. Happily for her, the campaign news goes on constantly thanks to cable television.

EPILOGUE

EDA AND EMILY AGAIN

At this juncture in Susan's life the everlasting ping-pong game Eda and Emily played has ended thanks to Aunt Emily's death. Susan's Mom, Eda, is 95 years old, and is senile and living in a nursing home in Florida. Susan would give a lot just to hear her criticize and gripe again. She had been such a vital life force. Second childhood as Shakespeare stated is sans mind, sans everything, and it is sad for Susan to watch. Eda not longer knows Susan and her cousins nor does she remember either of her husbands or even Emily. The net is down, and the ping pong game has ended. With Eda's death the curtain will descend on her generation of Susan's family. The Palm Sundays hopefully will continue.

ABOUT THE AUTHOR

Barto, Susan C. Born 6/21/41. Parents Eda and William Forcellon. Spouse: Harry W. Barto. Children: William M. Barto. Education: Katherine Gibbs School, Union College, New Jersey, Seton Hall, New Jersey. Extensive travel: Egypt, France, Italy, and England. Occupation: Legal Secretary, Legislative Aide, Writer last 20 years. Memberships: Past President Friends of the Hunterdon Museum of Art, Director of Volunteers at the Hunterdon Museum of Art, New Providence Library Board, New Providence, New Jersey, Raritan Valley College Book Group. Honors: Golden Certificate Awards, Drury's Publishing, Plaque of Appreciation from the New Providence Library Board, Listed in Who's Who in America 1999/2000 Who's Who in the East and 2000 Who's Who in America. Have been listed in numerous Who's Who's for all the past years since 2000 including 2007. Personal note: Married for 41 years to husband, Harry, who died in 2001. One son, William, who died in 2000.

I love to write. Writing defines who I am. Publishing Credits: Thirteen stories published by Creative With Words, 2 stories published by Writer's Guidelines and News. One story published in Yesterday's Magazette, One story published in a Reminisce hard cover book "The Fabulous Fifties", 3 stories published in Reminisce Magazine, and two stories published in Good Old Days Magazine. Many stories in Drury's anthologies and seven books of stories published by Drury's Publishing.

www.ingramcontent.com/pod-product-compliance
Lightning Source LLC
Chambersburg PA
CBHW051527050726
47503CB00014B/2192